house
farm

South
Downs

river

Ben's
house

Button
found here

Sky
found here

Chicken coop

Farmyard

Holly
found here

Jasmine's
house

Calf barn

Lucky
born here

To Roger Turner's farm →

Jasmine Green Rescues
A Donkey Called Mistletoe

Read all the books in the
JASMINE GREEN RESCUES series

Jasmine Green RESCUES
A Donkey Called Mistletoe

Helen Peters
illustrated by Ellie Snowdon

WALKER BOOKS

Text copyright © 2020 by Helen Peters
Illustrations copyright © 2020 by Ellie Snowdon

First US edition 2021
First published by Nosy Crow (UK) 2020

Library of Congress Catalog Card Number pending
ISBN 978-1-5362-2245-6 (hardcover)
ISBN 978-1-5362-2246-3 (paperback)

21 22 23 24 25 26 LBM 10 9 8 7 6 5 4 3 2 1

Printed in Melrose Park, IL, USA

This book was typeset in Bembo.
The illustrations were done in pencil with a digital wash overlay.

Walker Books US
a division of
Candlewick Press
99 Dover Street
Somerville, Massachusetts 02144

www.walkerbooksus.com

A JUNIOR LIBRARY GUILD SELECTION

For Kirsty and Fiona,
my wonderful editors
HP

For Han x
ES

1
The Back End of a Donkey

Jasmine and her best friend, Tom, were in the kitchen at Oak Tree Farm when Jasmine's little brother, Manu, flung the door open and ran in, dropping his coat and schoolbag on the floor.

"Guess what!" he said, an enormous grin on his face.

"What?" asked Jasmine, glancing up from the chopping board. She was cutting up a carrot as a treat for Dotty, the pet deer she had recently rescued and adopted. Dotty only had three legs, which meant she couldn't live in the wild, but she managed very well in the orchard.

"Where's Dad?" asked Manu. "I want to tell you all together."

"In his office," said Jasmine.

Their dad was the farmer at Oak Tree Farm. He worked outdoors most of the time but he had an office in the house where he did all his paperwork.

"Oh, good," said Manu, running out of the room. "I'll go get him. I've got the best news."

Jasmine's mom, Dr. Singh, walked into the kitchen and hung up her car keys. Mom was a vet, and she had picked up Manu from his after-school soccer club on her way home from the office.

"Hey, you two," she said. "I bet you're happy it's Friday."

"Yep," said Jasmine. "We're going to spend lots of time with Dotty and Truffle this weekend. Try to cheer them up."

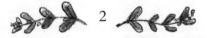

Truffle, Jasmine's pet pig, lived with Dotty in the orchard.

"Do you think they're any better today?" asked Mom.

"No," said Jasmine flatly. "They're still lying down all the time, and they've hardly touched their food."

Until last week, Jasmine's dad's elderly spaniel, Bramble, had lived in the orchard, too. But Bramble hadn't been very well for the past few months, and on Monday she had died in her sleep.

Mom had tried to comfort Jasmine. "She was very old for a spaniel. And she had a lovely life. She got to spend every day running around the farm with Dad, and when she wasn't with him she had Truffle and Dotty to keep her company."

But Jasmine was inconsolable. She was very upset about Bramble, but she was even sadder for Truffle and Dotty. They always used to run and greet her every time she came to see them. Truffle would grunt with happiness and flop over to have her tummy tickled. Dotty would lick Jasmine's hand and nuzzle against her. But since Bramble had passed, they just lay on the grass all day. Truffle kept her head down and Dotty curled herself up into a ball. They didn't even look up when Jasmine approached. Most worrying of all, they showed no interest in food.

"We're giving them carrots and grapes," Tom told Jasmine's mom. "We tried apples, but they didn't want them."

Just then, Manu came back, dragging Dad by the hand.

"So what's this amazing news, then?" asked Mom.

"We found out our parts in the annual nativity play," said Manu, "and guess what me and Ben are going to be?"

"Shepherds?" asked Mom.

Manu grinned and shook his head. "No."

"Wise Men?" asked Dad.

Jasmine snorted. "Wise Men? Those two? As if."

"Angels?" said Mom, and everybody laughed.

"Sheep?" suggested Tom.

Manu smiled knowingly. "Getting closer."

"Cows?" said Tom. "Pigs?"

Jasmine shook her head. "They're not clever enough to be pigs."

Manu could contain himself no longer. "We're the donkey!" he burst out.

Dad roared with laughter. "Well, that makes perfect sense."

 5

"Mrs. Cowan's going to get an actual donkey costume," said Manu, looking as if he might burst with excitement. "Ben's going to be the front legs and the head and I'm going to be the back legs."

"Well, this is definitely an event that will need to be recorded," said Dad. "We must make sure we get front-row seats."

"We're doing a special performance for the people at Holly Tree House the week before we do the one for the rest of the town. And we're going to have afternoon tea with the residents after the play," said Manu. "Everyone's going to sing 'Little Donkey' when me and Ben come in. Except Harrison. He won't sing. He doesn't even want to be in the play."

Harrison was a new boy in Manu's class. Manu and his best friend, Ben, had made friends with him right away. Jasmine's family had heard a lot about Harrison lately. Harrison was autistic and he liked things to be calm and orderly, so it was very strange, Jasmine thought, that Harrison would

6

want to be friends with her brother. But the boys had bonded over a shared love of bugs, and now they seemed to spend most of their recesses making homes for insects on the school field.

"Can Harrison come over?" asked Manu. "He says there'll be lots of good bugs here, because of all the dung."

"I like the sound of Harrison," said Dad. "Not everybody appreciates the finer qualities of farm manure."

"Of course he can come," said Mom. "I'll text his mother."

"Will Ella be home in time for the play?" asked Manu. "I really want her to see it."

Ella was Jasmine and Manu's older sister, and she was away at college.

"I'm sure she'll be there if she can," said Mom. "I can't believe my son's going to be the back end of a donkey. I've never been more proud."

 7

2
Meeting Mistletoe

On Saturday morning, Tom and Jasmine took grapes and pears out to the orchard. Truffle ate half-heartedly. Dotty just sniffed the pieces and turned away.

Jasmine sighed. "Look at her sad eyes. I don't think she'll ever feel better."

"It's only been a week," said Tom. "Your mom said they should improve soon."

"But what if they don't? What if they keep refusing to eat?"

"Do you think your dad will get another dog?" asked Tom.

Jasmine shook her head. "Manu wants a puppy, but Dad said no because of Sky."

Sky was a collie that Jasmine had rescued as a puppy. He belonged to her, but because he was a sheepdog, he spent a lot of time on the farm with Dad.

"And Mom says we've got more than enough pets as it is," said Jasmine.

As well as Truffle, Dotty, and Sky, Jasmine had two cats called Toffee and Marmite, a tame duck called Button, and a sheep called Lucky. Button lived with the chickens in the farmyard and Lucky lived with the other sheep in the field, though, so they didn't make any extra work.

When the children went in for lunch, Jasmine's dad said, "I'm going to do a few jobs for Mr. Hobson at Honey Farm this afternoon. Would you two like to come along?"

"Can we meet his donkey?" asked Jasmine.

"Of course," said Dad.

"Then we'll come," said Jasmine. "Won't we, Tom?"

"Definitely," said Tom.

Dad had told Jasmine about Mr. Hobson. He lived close to Oak Tree Farm. He was very old now, and Dad had recently started helping him out with odd jobs. Mr. Hobson had had to sell most of his animals, but he had kept Mistletoe, his pet donkey.

When they got to Honey Farm, Dad introduced Jasmine and Tom to the old farmer.

"Mistletoe's very friendly," Mr. Hobson said. "He'll love you making a fuss over him. Just approach him from the side, and talk to him as you approach so you don't startle him."

Jasmine and Tom left the adults to chat and walked across the yard to Mistletoe's field. Tom had brought a carrot for him and Jasmine had an apple, which they carried in their pockets. They stopped at the gate and scanned the field.

"There he is!" said Tom, pointing.

At the far end of the meadow, near a wooden barn, a small brown donkey was looking over the fence into the next field, where two floppy-eared goats and a group of hens were gathered.

"Come on," said Jasmine, climbing over the gate.

In the middle of the field, they passed a single tree. Its branches were bare, but a huge clump of mistletoe, with bright-green leaves and fat pearly-white berries, hung from a high branch.

"Look!" said Tom. "I wonder if that's how the donkey got his name."

"Hello, Mistletoe," said Jasmine as they slowly approached. "How are you today?"

Mistletoe had deep-brown eyes and a patient, gentle expression. His coat was all brown except for the tip of his nose, which was pure white, and a long black cross on his back.

"He's great," said Tom, stroking the donkey's dark mane. "He's got such a kind-looking face. And beautiful eyes."

 11

"He looks very thoughtful, doesn't he?" said Jasmine, patting Mistletoe's flank.

"Huge ears," said Tom, stroking the long pointed ears, brown on the outside and white on the inside, that stood straight up on the top of the donkey's head, facing attentively forward. Mistletoe nuzzled his arm.

"Look, he really likes me," said Tom.

Jasmine laughed. "I think he can smell the carrot."

Sure enough, the donkey started to nuzzle the pocket of Tom's coat. "You'll have to move your head away, Mistletoe," said Tom, "or I won't be able to get it."

Jasmine took the apple from her pocket and, holding it out with her palm flat, offered it to Mistletoe. He snatched it up and crunched noisily. When he finished, he started nuzzling Tom's pocket again. Tom held the carrot toward him. The donkey grabbed it and Tom hastily let go as Mistletoe pulled the whole thing into his mouth.

 13

He crunched it contentedly as Jasmine and Tom stroked his soft coat.

"He seems really peaceful," said Tom.

Suddenly Mistletoe lifted his head, pricked up his ears, and looked toward the farmyard. Jasmine and Tom followed his gaze and saw Mr. Hobson driving across the yard on his special all-terrain mobility scooter. The donkey brayed so loudly that Jasmine and Tom laughed in surprise. They followed him as he trotted to the gate to greet his friend.

Mr. Hobson opened the gate and drove into the field. The mobility scooter had big tires for driving across rough ground. Tom looked at it enviously.

Mistletoe put his nose in Mr. Hobson's lap. The farmer stroked him.

"How are you this morning, old boy? Have you been behaving yourself for these two?"

"He's been perfect," said Jasmine. "And he really liked the treats."

 14

Mr. Hobson laughed. "I bet he did. He loves his food, this one. He's getting too fat, having all this grass to himself."

"Does he like those goats and chickens?" asked Tom.

"He seems to. He spends a lot of time looking at them over the fence. I think he's been lonely since I had to sell the sheep. Donkeys are very sociable, so if they don't have another donkey around, they'll look for other animals to bond with."

"How old is he?" asked Tom.

"Nearly twenty. I've had him since he was a foal."

Tom looked alarmed. Bramble had been fifteen when she died.

Mr. Hobson saw the look on Tom's face. "Don't worry, twenty isn't that old for a donkey. They generally live to thirty, and some of them go on until fifty."

"Did you ever ride him?" asked Jasmine.

"No, I got him to protect the lambs against

 15

foxes. Donkeys are good guard animals for sheep. But he's always been more of a pet, really. And he's too old to start being ridden now."

"Is it true that all donkeys have a black cross on their backs?" asked Tom.

"Every donkey in the whole world. There's a legend that says it's because of their connection with Jesus. One version says the donkey that carried Jesus into Jerusalem on Palm Sunday went and stood beside him on his cross, and the shadow of the cross fell across the donkey's back and shoulders. But some scientists think it's for camouflage, the same way that tigers' stripes help them blend into their surroundings."

"He's so nice," said Tom, stroking Mistletoe's mane.

"He's the sweetest donkey you could ever hope to meet," said Mr. Hobson. "I'm really going to miss him."

"What do you mean?" asked Jasmine.

Mr. Hobson sighed. "I was just telling your dad.

It's gotten to the point where I can't look after him properly, and it's not fair to Mistletoe. I pay a girl to help out, but it's not much of a life for him. He loves company, and he's spending too much time on his own."

"So what are you going to do?" asked Jasmine.

"Well, I'm moving into Holly Tree House next month," said Mr. Hobson. Holly Tree House was an assisted-living place in town. "I've finally had to face the fact that I can't really manage on my own anymore. It's very nice of your dad and other people to come and help out, but they're all busy and I don't want to be a burden."

Jasmine couldn't think of anything to say. It seemed so awful that Mr. Hobson thought of himself as a burden.

"And Mistletoe will go to the animal sanctuary in Latchford," he said. "They phoned me this morning to say they can pick him up in two weeks."

"But isn't that miles away?" asked Tom.

 17

"It's a fair distance. I don't expect I'll ever see him again."

The old man looked so sad that Jasmine couldn't bear it.

"But me and Tom have an animal sanctuary," she said. "On our farm."

Mr. Hobson looked at her in surprise. So did Tom.

"Well, we do," said Jasmine, seeing Tom's look. "I mean, we're going to have an animal sanctuary when we're grown up. But we already do, really. We've rescued lots of animals."

This was true. As well as the animals that had stayed on the farm, Jasmine and Tom had rescued and then released or found homes for a baby goat, a kitten, and two sparrow chicks, along with an otter cub and a barn owl.

"But you're not allowed to have any more pets," said Tom.

Jasmine glared at him. "Yes, I am."

She smiled at Mr. Hobson. "Honestly, we'd

love to have Mistletoe. And then you could come and see him all the time."

Mr. Hobson patted her hand. "You're very kind, but you mustn't worry. I'm sure he'll be well looked after. Now, tell me all about your animals. Your dad says you've got a deer in the orchard. How's she doing?"

"She was doing really well until Dad's spaniel died last week. Bramble was like a mom to Dotty, and now Dotty's pining for her. So's Truffle, my pig. They all lived together, you see."

Jasmine and Tom talked with Mr. Hobson until they had to leave. As they walked to Dad's truck, Jasmine turned to look back at the old man and the donkey. Mistletoe had laid his head in Mr. Hobson's lap. Mr. Hobson was scratching Mistletoe's ears and speaking to him softly. And then Jasmine saw something that sent a stab of pain through her heart.

Mr. Hobson's eyes were full of tears.

3

A Donkey Sleepover

Back at Oak Tree Farm, Tom and Jasmine sat side by side on Jasmine's bed. She had her mom's laptop, and Tom had her dad's.

"We need to research everything about donkey care," she said. "Then we can show Mom and Dad we know all about donkeys and they'll let Mistletoe come and live here."

"But your parents won't let you have him. You just got Dotty, and they said no more animals."

"That's the whole point, though, isn't it?

Dotty and Truffle are missing Bramble, and Mistletoe will be missing Mr. Hobson. So they can all make friends, and then they'll cheer one another up."

Tom looked thoughtful. "That might work. He seemed to like those goats and chickens in the next field. OK, so let's find out how to look after donkeys."

The first thing he discovered was that, unlike horses, donkeys don't have a waterproof coat.

"So they need to be able to shelter from the rain. But there isn't a barn in the orchard, so he couldn't live with Dotty and Truffle."

Dotty and Truffle slept in Bramble's kennel. It was a big kennel, but not big enough for a donkey.

Jasmine was looking at Tom's screen. "It says a three-sided shelter is fine. Dad could build one. He's good at building stuff. And it could be my Christmas present."

Tom kept reading. "It says they should eat

22

mainly barley straw, because it's high in fiber and low in sugar, and it's close to what they would eat in the wild."

"That's perfect! We always have lots of barley straw for the cows and sheep."

"And they need a mineral block to lick."

"He's got one," said Jasmine. "I saw it in the barn. So we could take that with us. I could ask for another one for Christmas. The one he's got should last until then."

"Apart from that, they just need clean water, and they browse for food in the fields," said Tom. "It says it's good for them to share a field with other animals."

"For company?"

"Well, mainly because they get fat if they have too much grass. But they do need company, too, which is perfect for Dotty and Truffle."

Jasmine raised her eyebrows at him. "See, you like the idea now, don't you?"

"Well, it would be really nice having them

all living together. And donkeys don't seem that hard to look after."

"It says here they need their hooves trimmed by a farrier every six to ten weeks, to stop them from getting overgrown," said Jasmine. "I don't know how much that costs. But if I ask all my relatives for money for Christmas, hopefully I'll get enough to pay for the farrier's visits until my birthday."

Tom looked worried. "How are we actually going to do this, though? If Mistletoe's living in the orchard, we can't exactly keep it a secret for long."

"I'm not asking my parents," said Jasmine. "You know what they're like. They always say no to everything."

"So what are you going to do, then?"

"Mr. Hobson's happy for us to have him, isn't he? He said so."

Tom frowned. "No, he didn't."

"He said it was very kind of me to offer, but not to worry. That's what people say when they want you to do something but they're too polite to say so. Obviously he'd like us to have him."

"But we still can't keep him secretly."

"No, but we can bring him here without telling them first. And then he'll make friends with Dotty and Truffle, and once Mom and Dad see them all snuggled up happily together, they'll change their minds and let me keep him."

"But what if they don't? Or what if the animals don't like one another? Then we'd have to tell Mr. Hobson we couldn't keep him after all, and that wouldn't be fair."

 25

Jasmine sighed impatiently. But Tom was thinking. After a pause, he said, "How about we ask Mr. Hobson if we can bring Mistletoe here for a trial, to see how he gets along with the other animals? We could ask to bring him for just one night."

"Like a donkey sleepover!" said Jasmine.

"Exactly. Then once he's here, we can try to persuade your parents to let us keep him. And if they won't, then we'll just have to take him back and he'll go to the animal sanctuary, like Mr. Hobson's arranged anyway."

Jasmine nodded thoughtfully. "That is actually a good plan." She shut the laptop and stood up. "Let's find his number and phone him right now."

4
Withers and Fetlocks

Unfortunately, Mr. Hobson didn't think a donkey sleepover was a good idea. Not yet, anyway.

"Why don't you come and spend some time with him first?" he said. "I can show you what he needs and you can get to know him better."

"That would be great," said Jasmine, trying to hide her disappointment about the sleepover. "Can we come tomorrow?"

So they spent Sunday morning with Dotty and Truffle, and then walked across the fields to

Honey Farm after lunch. When they arrived, Mr. Hobson was in the field on his mobility scooter, stroking Mistletoe's neck.

"Thank you for helping out," he said. "I'm very grateful to you."

"We're very grateful to *you*," said Jasmine.

Mr. Hobson laughed. "You might not say that once you find out what you have to do. The first job is mucking out and picking up the dung."

"We don't mind," said Jasmine. "We want to do all the jobs."

Tom mucked out the barn while Jasmine trundled a wheelbarrow around the field, picking up dung with a manure scoop. She was hoping Mistletoe might follow her, but he stayed by Mr. Hobson's side the whole time.

When the children finished, Mr. Hobson said, "I imagine you'd like to groom him, wouldn't you?"

Jasmine and Tom grinned at each other.

"Can you bring his halter from the barn, then?"

 28

Jasmine fetched the halter and lead rope from the hook on the barn wall.

"He's used to wearing it," said Mr. Hobson, "but he needs to get used to you putting it on, so go slow. Talk to him quietly and take a bit of time to scratch his withers first, so he relaxes with you."

"Scratch his what?" said Tom.

Mr. Hobson indicated the point at the top of the donkey's shoulders, just below his mane.

"That's called his withers. Donkeys like being scratched there, and on their ears and back."

Jasmine scratched Mistletoe's withers while Tom stroked his ears.

"That's right," said Mr. Hobson. "You can see he's relaxed when he's standing nice and quietly like this and his ears are pointing forward. If he flattens his ears back, or swishes his tail or stamps his foot, those are all warning signs that he's uneasy about something."

"What should we do if he does that?" asked Tom.

29

"Just stand there quietly, and when he stops swishing or stamping, move away a bit. Never try to force a donkey to do anything. They respond to rewards, so if he does something well, stroke or scratch him."

"What about treats?" asked Jasmine.

Mr. Hobson shook his head. "Bribing donkeys with food encourages all sorts of bad behavior. They might just snatch it and run away, or even bite you to try to get a treat. The best reward is to give him attention. Now he's nice and relaxed, so you can hold the halter in front of him and let him sniff it."

Mistletoe happily sniffed the halter. Mr. Hobson showed the children how to adjust it and attach the lead rope to the ring under the donkey's chin.

"There you go. Now you can give him a scratch before you start grooming him."

"Do you groom him every day?" asked Jasmine.

"Generally we do. It's a good way to check for

any skin problems or injuries as well as keep him clean, and it helps you bond with him. We don't groom him if his coat's wet, though, because the water and dirt get to the skin, and that means more chance of infection."

Tom fetched the box of combs and brushes from the barn. Mr. Hobson placed it on his lap.

"Start with the dandy brush. One of you can hold the lead rope while the other one grooms him."

"You can brush him first if you want," Jasmine said to Tom, feeling very generous.

"Use the dandy brush to get dried mud and dirt off," said Mr. Hobson. "It's got hard bristles, so don't use it on his lower legs, face, or ears, where he's more sensitive."

Tom put his hand on Mistletoe's neck and said, "I'm just going to brush your back, OK?"

"That's exactly right," said Mr. Hobson approvingly. "Always keep a hand on him as you're working your way around so he knows where you are, and keep talking to him. And walk around the front of him, not the rear. He's very unlikely to kick, but you never know when something might startle him."

When Tom had finished, he held the rope while Jasmine used the soft-bristled body brush on Mistletoe's ears, face, belly, tail, and lower legs, talking reassuringly to him the whole time.

Mr. Hobson showed them how to clean the dirt out of the brushes with the plastic currycomb. Then he handed the hoof pick to Jasmine.

"His hooves need picking out every day. He's very quiet generally, but if he's in pain, or he senses you're nervous, he might kick, so go carefully. Start by running your hand from his withers down his front left shoulder, then down the back of his leg to the fetlock joint."

Jasmine wasn't sure what the fetlock joint was, so she ran her hand slowly down Mistletoe's leg, hoping Mr. Hobson would tell her where to stop. When her hand was almost at the bottom of the donkey's leg, Mr. Hobson said, "Now tug gently at the fetlock to encourage him to pick his foot up."

So a fetlock is basically an ankle, Jasmine thought.

She pulled gently. Mistletoe kept his foot on the ground. She tried again but he still didn't budge.

"If he doesn't want to move, lean against his shoulder with your hip," said Mr. Hobson. "That

33

usually does the trick. It shifts his weight to the other foot, you see."

Jasmine leaned heavily against Mistletoe and grasped his fetlock again. This time, he picked up his foot.

Good," said Mr. Hobson. "Now, don't lift it too high, and keep his foot directly under his body—you don't want to put any strain on his joints."

Following Mr. Hobson's instructions, Jasmine picked out the mud and small stones from Mistletoe's front feet. Then she held the rope while Tom did the back ones.

"If you do that every day," said Mr. Hobson, "you get to know how his feet should look, and you'll be able to spot any injuries or swelling early on."

"It's so much work looking after a donkey," said Tom in amazement. "I always thought they just lived in a field and that was it."

Mr. Hobson smiled. "Are you changing your minds?"

"No!" they said, shaking their heads emphatically.

Tom was right, Jasmine thought. It was a lot of work. But that just made it more exciting. She couldn't wait to take Mistletoe home with her.

5
One Crucial Question

When Tom and Jasmine had finished grooming Mistletoe, Mr. Hobson showed them how to lead him around the field on a slack rope. They had to say "Walk on" when they wanted him to move and "Halt" to get him to stop.

Jasmine was getting more and more excited at the thought of bringing Mistletoe to Oak Tree Farm. But first there was one crucial question to be answered: Would Mistletoe get along with Dotty and Truffle?

As they unfastened his halter, Jasmine had an idea.

"Would it be OK to come again next Saturday and bring Dotty with us? To introduce her to Mistletoe?"

Mr. Hobson smiled at her. "Is this part of your scheme to have Mistletoe live at your farm?"

"Yes. He'd be living in the orchard with Dotty and Truffle, you see."

"And what do your mom and dad think about this?"

"I haven't exactly told them yet," said Jasmine. "We want to make sure the animals get along first."

"Well, by all means bring Dotty on Saturday. I'd love to meet her."

"Can we bring my dog as well? He's very well behaved."

"Of course. I'd love to meet him, too."

"It's just that Dotty's so depressed at the moment, she might refuse to come on her own. But if Sky's coming, she'll probably come, too."

 37

"Why don't you make a little pen for the deer?" said Mr. Hobson. "Then she and Mistletoe can get to know each other, but she'll be safe if Mistletoe doesn't like her for any reason."

Tom and Jasmine fetched four metal rails from the farmyard and constructed a little pen at the edge of the field. Jasmine called Mistletoe over to join them, but instead he walked to Mr. Hobson and nuzzled into his shoulder. Mr. Hobson leaned his head against the donkey's and closed his eyes.

A horrible wave of guilt flooded over Jasmine. She had been so excited about having Mistletoe that she had barely thought about how sad it would be for him and Mr. Hobson to be parted. How selfish she felt.

She was still feeling terrible when her mom and Manu appeared at the gate.

"Why are you here?" asked Jasmine.

"Well that's a lovely greeting," said Mom. "Tom's going to his auntie's house, and I have to go shopping, so I said I'd pick you both up."

They dropped Tom at his auntie's house and then drove to the supermarket. Jasmine and Manu wanted to go to the toy aisle, but Mom steered them toward the food.

"Right, Manu, I need you to behave yourself," said Mom as they headed toward the fruit and vegetable aisle. "No sneaking things into the cart, OK?"

"Can I get extra carrots?" asked Jasmine. "For Dotty and Truffle?"

"Sure," said Mom. "But just get the cheap ones."

While Mom was choosing vegetables, Manu darted into the candy aisle, snatched an enormous chocolate bar from the shelf, and slipped it into the cart, covering it with a bag of potatoes.

 39

"Take that out of the cart, Manu," said Mom as they turned into the next aisle.

"How did you even see that?" said Manu.

"Just go put it back on the shelf."

"*Please*, Mom," said Manu. "You never let us buy fun stuff. Everyone else is allowed to—"

"No arguing," said Mom. "Put it back, please."

"Oh, look, it's Harrison!" said Manu.

Harrison's mom was pushing her shopping cart slowly down the aisle, scanning the shelves. Harrison walked beside her. He was wearing headphones and reading a book.

"Hey, Harrison!" called Manu.

"He won't hear you with headphones on," said Jasmine.

But Harrison looked up and gave Manu a little wave.

"See?" said Manu triumphantly. "His headphones just make things quieter, but he can still hear. They're really cool. I've tried them."

He walked over to his friend. Harrison's mom smiled at Manu.

"Jasmine, can you take that chocolate back, please?" said Mom. "I need to speak to Sarah."

When Jasmine returned, the moms were arranging for Harrison to visit the farm next weekend, and Harrison was telling Manu about his book.

"Did you know a bee's wings beat more than two hundred times per second?" said Harrison. "That's why they make such a loud buzzing sound."

"Wow," said Manu. "I thought they made the buzzing sound with their mouths."

"The queen bee can lay twenty-five hundred eggs a day in the summer," said Harrison. "Look."

Manu leaned over Harrison's shoulder to look at a large diagram of a bee.

"Mom," he said, tugging at his mom's sleeve. "Did you know a honeybee has five eyes? That's so cool!"

Harrison's mom smiled. "I can see why these two get along."

"I hope Manu isn't too noisy for him," said Mom.

"Harrison doesn't mind," said Sarah. "He likes making bug habitats with Manu and Ben. He just walks away if they get to be too much for him."

"I don't blame him," said Jasmine. "That's what I do, too."

6
Getting to Know Each Other

On the following Saturday afternoon, Jasmine and Tom set out for Honey Farm with Dotty and Sky. The collie bounded across the fields, wagging his tail and running in big circles around the children. Dotty walked on her lead beside Jasmine. As Jasmine had predicted, the deer had been reluctant to come. So reluctant, in fact, that Jasmine had had to carry Dotty out of the orchard while Sky leaped around her and gave the deer some encouraging barks and licks.

Mr. Hobson and Mistletoe were at the far end of the field when they arrived. Tom tied Sky to the gatepost outside. "Good boy," he said. "Stay there."

Sky lay down contentedly, and Jasmine led Dotty to the pen. Mr. Hobson drove across the field to greet them.

"What a beautiful little deer," he said, stroking Dotty's face. "She's a real credit to you, Jasmine."

"Thank you," said Jasmine, gazing at Dotty with pride. "She's too skinny at the moment, though. She hasn't been eating well since Bramble died."

"Should we bring Mistletoe to meet her?" asked Tom.

Mr. Hobson shook his head. "Best to let him do it in his own time."

So Jasmine got on with the mucking-out and Tom did the poop-picking, while Mistletoe browsed in the hedge at the top of the field. Dotty stood at the rails of the pen, making

 44

her little bleating call to Jasmine now and again. Jasmine hoped Mistletoe would want to meet Dotty, but he didn't even seem to have noticed her.

Just as they finished their jobs, a middle-aged man walked into the field. He wore very new-looking jeans with nice shoes and a flowery shirt. He didn't look like a farmer.

"Dad!" he called, and Mr. Hobson turned and drove across the field to meet him. Jasmine and Tom stared in fascination at Mr. Hobson's son. He looked so different from his father.

Jasmine couldn't hear what Mr. Hobson's son said, but she did hear Mr. Hobson say, "Yes, that's fine. Do what you like with it. Don't fuss, I'll be in later."

His son said something else that Jasmine couldn't hear, and then he strode back toward the house, frowning. Jasmine glanced at Tom, and she could tell he felt awkward, too.

They walked over to Mr. Hobson.

45

"If you need to go in, it's OK," said Jasmine. "We know what to do now."

He smiled at her. "I know you do. But it's a good excuse to keep out of the way while my children pack up the house. I've told them I don't care about any of it except the books and pictures, but they keep fussing."

"Look!" whispered Tom.

Mistletoe had left the hedge and was ambling toward Dotty's pen. Jasmine held her breath as the old donkey approached the rails and stared at the little deer. Dotty stared back at him for several seconds. Then she leaned her long neck toward him until their faces were nearly touching. She sniffed. Mistletoe sniffed back.

Mr. Hobson smiled. "That's good. They're getting to know each other."

The children walked Sky around the edge of the field on his leash, to give Dotty and Mistletoe time to bond. When they got back to Dotty's pen, Mistletoe had his head over the rails. They watched as Dotty leaned toward him and licked the side of his nose. The donkey stretched his head farther into the pen and Dotty licked him again.

"They've started bonding!" said Jasmine. "Do you think we could let Dotty out of the pen?"

"Try it," said Mr. Hobson. "I think they'll get along fine."

Jasmine opened the pen and put on Dotty's lead. To her surprise and delight, Mistletoe turned and walked beside them as she led Dotty across the field. Tom and Sky walked on the other side of Mistletoe.

"Why don't you let Sky have a run off the leash?" suggested Mr. Hobson. "He and Mistletoe don't seem bothered by each other."

Sky was delighted to be free. He bounded around the field, sniffing at every new scent, his tail wagging in delight. Mistletoe stayed with Dotty.

"Let the deer off the lead, too, if you like," said Mr. Hobson. So they did, but Dotty didn't run off like Sky. She stayed next to Mistletoe, matching his pace. She looked happier than she had since Bramble had died.

"That's amazing," said Tom. "She's attached to him already."

"I think she can sense something in Mistletoe that's like Bramble," said Jasmine. "Like Mistletoe has the same sort of soul as Bramble. Calm and gentle."

"Perhaps she likes being with an older animal," said Mr. Hobson. "Like a sort of parent figure."

"Do you know if Mistletoe gets along with pigs? He'd be living with Truffle, too."

"I don't think he's ever met a pig. But I've never had a problem with him getting along with any animal."

"I don't think we can bring Truffle here, though," said Jasmine. "She used to go for walks when she was younger, but she doesn't anymore."

"How about you take Mistletoe to your place, then?" asked Mr. Hobson. "For your sleepover thing. Practice a bit more with him on the lead now, then you should be fine to walk him over the fields tomorrow."

Tom and Jasmine beamed in delight. "That would be amazing!" said Jasmine.

"You'll have to ask your parents first, though," said Mr. Hobson. "I don't want them getting angry with me for letting you take a donkey home without their permission."

7

Like a Bucking Bronco

"Ted Hobson phoned to say how helpful you and Tom have been," said Dad at dinnertime. "Sounds like he's enjoyed having you around."

Jasmine knew a good chance when she saw it. "He said we can walk Mistletoe over here tomorrow. It's very good for donkeys to go for walks and get new stimulation."

Mom frowned. "Are you sure you'll be able to manage him by yourselves?"

Manu looked excited. "Me and Ben can

practice his walk and copy his noises, and then when we get the costume we'll be exactly like a real donkey."

"Can we ride him, too?" asked Ben, who had come to have dinner with Manu.

Manu's eyes lit up. "Let's have a rodeo! If I got on him and kicked my heels, I bet he'd gallop."

"You can't ride him," said Jasmine. "He's old and he's never been ridden. He might throw you off."

Ben laughed. "Like a bucking bronco!"

"He couldn't throw *me* off," said Manu, "even if he got right up on his hind legs. I'd just hold on to his mane, and even if he was kicking and going wild, I wouldn't fall off."

"You fell off the bucking bronco at the school fair," said Ben. "You only stayed on it for about two seconds."

"That wasn't my fault. The man didn't give me a chance to get on properly before he started it up."

"You fell off on your second try, too. And your third. And—"

"Anyway, you're not riding him," said Jasmine, "so don't even think about it." She turned to her father. "Dad, can me and Tom fence off a bit of the orchard?"

"What for?"

"Just so Mistletoe can rest there. We don't want to leave him tied up, but we can't let him loose with Truffle, in case they don't get along. He's going to be here all day while Mr. Hobson's clearing out his house."

"Poor Mr. Hobson," said Mom. "It must be terrible, having to leave his home."

"Especially when he's leaving Mistletoe, too," said Jasmine. "And the animal sanctuary's so far away that they won't ever see each other again."

Mom gave her a stern look. "I know what you're trying to do, Jasmine, but you know perfectly well what the answer is."

"I thought Dotty was looking more perky

 53

this afternoon," said Dad, trying to change the subject.

"That's because we took her to see Mistletoe," said Jasmine. "You wouldn't believe how well they get along. Imagine how happy she'd be if he could stay here forever."

Jasmine felt tremendous pride as they led the old donkey across the fields on Sunday morning. He walked calmly beside them, his ears forward. Tom held the lead rope and Jasmine carried the box of brushes and equipment.

"He really trusts us, doesn't he?" said Tom. "He's quite happy with us leading him."

Dad had helped them put a fence across the orchard. Dotty and Truffle were in the top half, and the children led Mistletoe through the garden gate into the bottom half. They had filled a feed bowl with fresh barley straw.

"He'll love browsing in the hedge," said Jasmine. "There's so much tasty stuff there."

Dotty and Truffle were lying under an apple tree. As Mistletoe walked into the orchard, Dotty raised her head. She gave an excited bleat and scrabbled to her feet. Mistletoe brayed in greeting and Tom unclipped the lead rope.

The fence was no barrier for the little deer. She leaped over it easily and ran toward the donkey. She stopped in front of him and he dipped his head so she could nuzzle his face.

"What a lovely sight!"

Tom and Jasmine turned to see Mom standing at the gate.

Jasmine beamed. "See how they love each other. We think Dotty's adopted Mistletoe as a kind of replacement for Bramble."

Dotty set off at a trot around the orchard. To Jasmine's amazement, Mistletoe started to trot after her.

"Look how happy they are! And Dotty's been so miserable. It's like they were made for each other."

Mom sighed. "They're very sweet together. I can absolutely see that. But you can't just keep accumulating animals forever."

"Why not?"

"Well, for one thing, the expense. There's the cost of putting up a decent shelter. And donkeys need regular farrier's visits, did you know that?"

"Yes," said Jasmine. "I'm going to ask everyone for money for Christmas and birthdays. And—"

Mom's phone rang. She took it out of her pocket and looked at the screen.

"Sorry, I need to get this. But the answer is still no." She walked back toward the house.

"She's not going to change her mind, is she?" said Tom. "I mean, if she wasn't even convinced by seeing them together like that, what will it take to convince her?"

Mistletoe and Dotty spent the whole morning together, grazing and browsing, occasionally kicking up their heels and going for a trot around the orchard. Jasmine kept hoping that Mistletoe and Truffle would start to make friends, but they took no notice at all of each other.

Manu was very excited to meet Mistletoe, but he soon grew restless when the donkey wasn't as lively as he'd hoped.

"Why doesn't he gallop? I thought he'd be galloping all the time."

"He's an old donkey," said Jasmine. "And it's not a rodeo."

"He's a boring donkey," said Manu.

He left the orchard. A few minutes later, he was back. "Mom wants you in the kitchen."

Jasmine frowned. "What for?"

"Dunno. She said she needs to talk to you right now. And Tom."

Tom looked worried. "What have we done?"

"I don't know," said Jasmine. Her mind went over all her recent crimes. "Maybe she knows it was us who ate that whole package of cookies. But she doesn't usually make a fuss about stuff like that."

Mom was in the kitchen working on her laptop.

"What did you want us for?" asked Jasmine.

Mom looked up, a puzzled expression on her face. "What do you mean?"

"Manu said you wanted to see us."

Mom frowned. "I didn't say that."

At the exact same moment, Tom and Jasmine gasped. They stared at each other, each seeing their own thoughts mirrored in the other's face. Without a word, they turned and ran.

It was exactly as Jasmine had feared. As soon as they came within sight of the orchard, she saw Manu trying to scramble onto Mistletoe. He was almost across the donkey's back, and he was frantically trying to hoist himself upright. Mistletoe's ears were flattened back, and he was swishing his tail and stamping.

For a moment, Jasmine stood frozen in panic. Then she started running, her heart thumping in her chest, praying Mistletoe wouldn't bolt before she got to Manu. As she reached the orchard gate, Manu started slithering off Mistletoe's back. In a desperate attempt to stay on, he grabbed the donkey's mane in both fists. Mistletoe threw up his head and brayed loudly. He kicked up his heels and galloped across the orchard. Manu screamed as his feet dragged across the grass, one of his hands still clutching Mistletoe's mane.

Jasmine raced into the orchard. But before she could reach Manu, Mom, with what seemed like superhuman speed, sprinted past her.

"Let go!" Mom shouted, running alongside Mistletoe and grabbing Manu around the waist. "I've got you!"

Manu let go and Mom pulled him away. The donkey continued to gallop around the orchard, braying and tossing his head. Mom led Manu into the garden. Jasmine followed, shutting the gate

 60

behind her. Manu was wide-eyed and his teeth were chattering.

"What is wrong with you?" Jasmine shouted. "I told you not to ride Mistletoe!"

Jasmine felt tears prickling at her eyelids. Manu had ruined everything. She would never be allowed to keep Mistletoe now.

8
Harrison Meets Mistletoe

However much Jasmine protested, Mom wouldn't budge.

"It's just not safe. You can't watch him all the time, and then there's your brother. You have to take Mistletoe back to Honey Farm."

"But that's so unfair!"

"I'm sorry, Jasmine, but we can't trust Manu around him. And Harrison's coming this afternoon. Manu might take him into the orchard, and

I'm not risking Harrison getting kicked in the head by a donkey."

"He wouldn't! Mistletoe's the sweetest donkey ever. He just got spooked by Manu trying to ride him. And he didn't even do anything bad. He just tried to get away from Manu, which is totally understandable."

"Maybe," said Mom. "But I'm responsible for Harrison while he's here and I can't take the risk."

"So we have to take him back right now?"

"Well, not this minute. He needs to calm down first. But you or Tom must be in the orchard the entire time, OK? And Manu, you are not allowed in there under any circumstances."

"I wouldn't anyway," Manu said. "That donkey's vicious. And he's got fleas."

"He does not," said Jasmine indignantly.

"He *does*, look. They bit me all over. It's really itchy."

Mom, Tom, and Jasmine turned to Manu.

Although it was November, he had insisted on dressing in shorts and a T-shirt. And his bare arms and legs were covered in big blotchy purple lumps.

"Oh, my goodness, Manu, you must be allergic," said Mom.

"Allergic to donkeys?"

"It looks like it. Try not to scratch. I'll give you some antihistamine to stop the itching. And you definitely can't touch Mistletoe again."

"I'm not going to," said Manu. "He's evil."

When Harrison arrived, he and Manu went out to the garden to make a bug habitat. Tom had to go home, but he was coming back later to walk Mistletoe to Honey Farm. Mom gave Jasmine strict instructions not to leave the orchard.

Mistletoe had calmed down now. He and Dotty were browsing in the hedge at the bottom of the orchard. His ears were facing forward and his muscles were relaxed.

Jasmine trundled her wheelbarrow around,

picking up manure. In the garden, Manu was digging a hole with a big spoon. Harrison had lost interest in digging. He stood in front of a bush away from Manu, craning his head forward to look intently at something on a leaf.

Truffle heaved herself up from where she had been lying under an apple tree. She shook her head and flapped her huge floppy ears. Mistletoe turned toward her and brayed softly. He and Truffle hadn't bonded yet, but they certainly didn't seem to mind each other.

Not that it matters anymore, thought Jasmine miserably. *There's no chance of Mistletoe coming to live here now. Next week he'll be taken to the animal sanctuary, and none of us will ever see him again.*

When Harrison heard Mistletoe bray, he looked up from the leaf he was studying. His eyes fell on the donkey. He stood completely still, watching him.

Jasmine carried on pushing the wheelbarrow, glancing regularly at Harrison, whose attention was still fixed on Mistletoe. She didn't think Harrison would do anything to upset the donkey, but she had promised Mom she would be super careful.

She stopped by the hedge to scoop up some dung.

"Is that your donkey?" asked Harrison.

The question made Jasmine sad. If only she could say yes!

"No," she said. "He belongs to someone else, but I'm looking after him today. He's called Mistletoe."

"Mistletoe," Harrison murmured. He continued to look at the donkey for a minute. Then he said, "Can I pet him?"

Jasmine hesitated. Would Mom be mad if she let Harrison come into the orchard? But Mistletoe was such a gentle donkey. If Manu hadn't tried to ride him, there wouldn't have been any trouble.

"OK," she said. "Just walk slowly and talk to him quietly. He likes people to be calm around him."

Harrison opened the gate and walked slowly down the orchard, keeping close to the hedge, watching Mistletoe, who was grazing in the far corner. When Harrison reached the bottom of the orchard, he stood still, looking intently at the donkey on the opposite side.

Mistletoe appeared to be grazing, but Jasmine could see that this was what Mr. Hobson had called "sham grazing." He was only pretending to eat the grass. His eyes were trained on Harrison.

After a while, Mistletoe lifted his head and started to amble toward the boy. He stopped in front of him and looked straight at him. Harrison returned his gaze. The boy and the donkey stood completely still, looking into each other's eyes.

"Hello, Mistletoe," said Harrison softly.

He reached out and touched the donkey's face. Slowly and gently, he began to stroke him, speaking softly to him as he did so. Jasmine could tell that Mistletoe was listening. His ears were pointed toward Harrison and his body language was relaxed.

For several minutes, Harrison stood there, speaking softly and stroking the donkey's face and ears. Then Mistletoe bent and sniffed Harrison's shoes. Harrison giggled. Mistletoe's ears flattened and he took a step backward. Harrison stood rigid, looking anxious. He waited a few seconds and then he took another step toward the donkey. Mistletoe stayed still as Harrison reached out and stroked him.

A slow smile spread over Harrison's face. He leaned his forehead in to touch the donkey's forehead. Jasmine tensed, watching Mistletoe. But he looked completely relaxed, his breathing slow and gentle. He and Harrison stayed leaning toward each other, their foreheads touching, for several silent seconds. Then Mistletoe gently lifted his head and started to amble across the orchard. Harrison fell into step beside him, and Mistletoe kept one ear trained on the boy as they walked side by side.

"You say 'Walk on' when you want him to move, and 'Stand' when you want him to stop," Jasmine said.

Mistletoe stopped to graze by the dividing fence, a few yards away from Jasmine. Harrison stroked the donkey's back, saying his name softly as he petted him.

 69

"He likes that," said Jasmine. "You can brush his coat if you want."

Harrison nodded. Jasmine fetched the halter and the box of brushes and combs.

"This is the dandy brush," she said, taking it from the box. "It's got stiff bristles, so we don't use it on his face or legs. There's another one with softer bristles for the parts where he's more sensitive."

Harrison didn't look at Jasmine, but he took the brush and examined it closely, stroking his fingers over the bristles.

Jasmine showed Harrison the halter and explained what she was doing as she let Mistletoe sniff it before she put it on. Once the donkey was wearing the halter and lead rope, she said, "There, you can brush his back now if you want to."

Harrison stroked the brush gently down Mistletoe's back.

"Good," said Jasmine. "See how he's standing quiet and relaxed, with his ears pointing forward. That means he likes you brushing him."

A car appeared on the farm driveway. Jasmine glanced around and saw it was Harrison's dad. Harrison didn't seem to have noticed. He was absorbed in brushing Mistletoe with slow, rhythmic strokes.

He brushed Mistletoe's back thoroughly on both sides, and then, without looking at her, he handed the brush back to Jasmine.

"Do you want the soft brush now?" she asked. Harrison nodded and held out his hand.

Jasmine noticed that her mom and Harrison's dad were watching them over the garden gate. Mom shot Jasmine a look, and Jasmine knew she was about to be in big trouble. But just as Mom made a move to open the gate, Harrison's dad said something that changed her mind. The two adults stood still, watching the children.

Jasmine handed Harrison the body brush. "This is for his face, ears, tail, and legs."

Harrison inspected it carefully. Then he brushed the donkey gently and rhythmically. As he bent down to groom the lower legs, Jasmine watched for any stamping or tail swishing, but Mistletoe stayed calm.

Harrison kept his eyes fixed on the donkey as

he handed the brush back to Jasmine. Then he pointed to the halter.

"We can take it off now," said Jasmine.

As soon as Mistletoe was free, he walked off toward Dotty. Harrison followed him, but he stumbled on a clump of grass and fell.

To her amazement, Mistletoe stopped and turned. He lowered his head to the boy's as Harrison lay on the ground, and sniffed Harrison's hair. Harrison laughed softly and said, "Mistletoe."

He put out his hand to stroke the donkey's face, and then he got to his feet and the two of them walked down the orchard together.

Jasmine turned and saw Harrison's dad watching, mesmerized.

He caught her eye and smiled. "Thank you so much. That was amazing to watch. I've never seen him so relaxed with an animal."

"Well, Mistletoe is very special," said Jasmine.

 73

Harrison's dad nodded. "There's something very peaceful about him, isn't there? He's so calm that he seems to calm Harrison down, too."

"And Harrison understands Mistletoe," said Jasmine. "He knows Mistletoe likes to be approached quietly and spoken to softly. Mistletoe really liked Harrison talking to him."

When his dad told Harrison it was time to go, Harrison ignored him and kept petting Mistletoe.

"You can come and see him again," said Jasmine. "And groom him, if you like."

Harrison's face broke into a beaming smile.

It was only after Harrison and his dad had left the orchard that Jasmine remembered Mistletoe wouldn't be coming back.

9
A Tattered Brown Envelope

Harrison's mom phoned the following Saturday morning as Jasmine and her parents were having breakfast. Manu had already left to spend the day with Ben.

"Sarah said Harrison was happy all day after he met Mistletoe," said Mom when she got off the phone. "They asked him why he likes Mistletoe so much, and he said it's because he's kind and his coat is soft. Sarah said he had the best night's sleep he's had in months."

"Well, it's nice that *some* people appreciate Mistletoe," said Jasmine, pouring syrup over her pancake, "instead of banning him from the farm and sending him to an orphanage."

"A sanctuary," said Dad. "And we're not sending him. He's not ours to send."

"Sarah asked if Harrison could come again next weekend," said Mom. "I had to tell her that Mistletoe wouldn't be here."

"That's a shame," said Jasmine, glancing at her

mom. Was it her imagination, or did Mom sound a bit regretful?

"Harrison and Mistletoe were forming a real bond," said Jasmine. "It would have been nice for Harrison to see him more. And Dotty was getting so much better, and Truffle was starting to bond with him, too. They'll be really depressed again now."

"All right, Jasmine, that's enough," said Mom.

"And poor Mr. Hobson," Jasmine continued. "It will probably break his heart. If Mistletoe lived here, we could bring Mr. Hobson to visit. But now they'll never see each other again, all because of you and your meanness."

"Jasmine, you've got a pig and a deer in the orchard already," said Mom. "Now you want a donkey. What next? Am I going to look out of the window one morning and see a giraffe grazing in the garden?"

"That would be so cool. Where can I get a giraffe?"

Mom ignored this. "Donkeys have very long lives, you know. They can live until they're fifty."

"What are you saying? That I should only have pets with short life spans in case I get bored with them?"

"No, of course not. You're wonderful at looking after your animals. However awful the weather is, however tired you are, you never neglect them."

"So what's the problem, then? Because you can't say it's because of Manu anymore."

Mom and Dad had had a talk with Manu about Mistletoe. What with the fright he had suffered when Mistletoe had bolted and the nastiness of his allergic reaction, he was adamant that he wanted nothing more to do with the donkey. And for once, they all believed him.

"Well, for one thing, we don't have infinite space or money," said Dad.

"We've got plenty of space for a donkey. And Mistletoe can be my Christmas present. Which is great for you, because he's free. You'd actually be

 78

making money. His equipment must be worth a lot. He only needs food, and we have that already."

"And a stable."

"A three-sided shelter is fine. It doesn't have to be fancy."

"It's still expensive. It needs flooring and electricity, for a start."

"And then there's the farrier's visits," said Mom. "And he'll need regular dental treatment, especially given his age."

The doorbell rang. "That'll be Tom," said Jasmine, standing up. "We're taking Dotty and Sky to see Mistletoe. We need to make the most of it since you're sending him away on Monday."

The next day was Jasmine's final day with Mistletoe. Mom and Dad were going to help Mr. Hobson clear out his farm buildings, so they gave her a lift to Honey Farm. Dotty and Sky rode in the back of the truck. Manu came along to help, though Jasmine had serious doubts about how much use he would be. Tom had to go visit his cousins, so he had said a sad goodbye to Mistletoe yesterday.

Mr. Hobson was in the donkey's field when they arrived. Manu's eyes lit up at the sight of the mobility scooter.

"That is so cool," he said as Mr. Hobson drove toward them, Mistletoe walking beside him. "I want one."

"You can have one," said Dad. "Once you need it."

Mr. Hobson greeted them all warmly. "You must be so proud of Jasmine," he said. "She's a natural with Mistletoe. He's really enjoyed having her and Tom around. And he loves young Dotty, too. He's like a foal again when he's with her."

Mistletoe bent to sniff Dotty's nose.
Then Dotty set off at a run, and Mistletoe
trotted after her. Sky ran along the hedgerow,
sniffing for rabbits.

Jasmine headed to the barn to muck it out.
When she finished, she was surprised to see
Mom and Dad still talking with Mr. Hobson.

Manu had clearly gotten bored and was poking around in the hedge with a stick. Mistletoe had returned to Mr. Hobson's side, and Dotty was grazing beside him.

Jasmine fetched the halter and lead rope. "Should I tie him to the holding ring in the barn while I groom him?" she asked.

"No, I'll hold the rope," said Mr. Hobson. "I want to spend as much time as I can with him today."

He reached up to scratch Mistletoe behind the ears. The donkey leaned his head toward him. For a few moments, the old man and the donkey stayed completely still, their eyes closed and their heads touching.

Jasmine felt tears prickle her eyes. She couldn't bear to think of Mistletoe being loaded up into a trailer and driven away.

She glanced at her parents. They looked sad, too. *They should be,* she thought.

Eventually her dad broke the silence. "Is it just

the granary that needs clearing out, Ted? Or is there anything else you want to get rid of?"

"Probably best if I come and show you," said Mr. Hobson. "Will you be all right for a minute, Jasmine? I'll be back shortly."

"Sure," said Jasmine. "I'll poop-pick the field."

"Are you coming with us, Manu?" asked Dad.

But Manu had found a gap big enough to crawl into and was busy exploring the hollow section in the middle of the hedge.

Mr. Hobson hadn't returned when Jasmine finished, so she put Mistletoe's halter on him and tied the rope to the ring outside the barn. By the time she had groomed the donkey, Mr. Hobson still hadn't returned, so she untied Mistletoe and played with Sky while Mistletoe and Dotty grazed together.

It was lunchtime, and she was beginning to feel very hungry, when she heard Mr. Hobson's scooter approaching the gate. Her parents walked beside him.

 83

"Are you finished?" she asked as they came toward her.

"We've barely started," said Dad. "We got a bit caught up talking."

Mr. Hobson smiled at Jasmine. He reached into the pocket of his tweed jacket.

"Here you are," he said, handing her a tattered brown envelope.

"What is it?"

"Open it and see," he said, his eyes sparkling.

Jasmine pulled out a small blue booklet. Stamped on the cover in silver lettering were the words:

DONKEY BREED SOCIETY
EQUINE PASSPORT

"You'll need to get it updated within thirty days," said Mr. Hobson, "with the new owner's details."

Jasmine stared at him. Then she stared at her

 84

parents. They were smiling. Did this really mean what she hoped it meant?

"That means your details, Jasmine," said Mom.

"My . . . ? You mean . . . ?"

"Yes. I know we've been resisting, but we completely trust you to put in the work. And you clearly have a talent for working with donkeys."

Jasmine felt dazed. "I can keep Mistletoe?"

"You can keep Mistletoe," said Dad. "Mr. Hobson's already phoned the sanctuary to let them know. You're his owner now."

A wave of joy surged over Jasmine. "Oh, thank you! Thank you so much."

"Thank Mr. Hobson, not us. He persuaded us to let you have him, and he's insisted on paying for the shelter."

Jasmine turned to Mr. Hobson. "Oh, you shouldn't do that," she began, but he held up his hand to stop her.

"I insisted. It was breaking my heart to think of being parted from Mistletoe forever. It's lovely to know he'll be staying in town. And he couldn't be in better hands."

"He'll still be your donkey, too," said Jasmine. "You can come and see him every week. He belongs to both of us now."

10
A Surprise

Dad built a shelter in the orchard, and when Mr. Hobson moved to Holly Tree House, Mistletoe moved to Oak Tree Farm. Right from the start, Dotty slept in the new shelter with the donkey. And on the third morning after Mistletoe's arrival, Jasmine was thrilled to see Truffle there, too, lying on her side in the straw, looking utterly content. That afternoon, Jasmine took away the dividing fence. There was no need for it anymore; the animals were perfectly happy together.

The following Saturday was the day of the nativity play at Holly Tree House. Manu was in a state of high excitement.

"Finally," he said through a mouthful of cereal. "Finally we get to wear the donkey costume. We're going to be the best donkey ever. And we're swapping so I can be the front end."

"How come?" asked Dad.

"Because I wanted to have the head on, and Ben said he wanted to be the back legs anyway, because donkeys kick with their back legs. I bet they kick with their front legs, too, though."

Mom and Dad shot each other alarmed looks.

"You will be careful in the donkey costume, won't you?" said Mom.

"Of course I will. I'm always careful."

Jasmine was excited, too, but for a different reason. Mr. Hobson was coming to visit Mistletoe

for the first time this morning. Mom was going to pick him
up from Holly Tree House.

"It's going to be a busy day for Mr. Hobson,"
said Dad, "with a visit in the morning and a play
in the afternoon."

Jasmine and Tom had decorated the shelter
with tinsel and strings of lights. They groomed
Mistletoe until his coat shone.

"There," Tom said, putting down the brush. "Mr. Hobson's going to be so happy to see you again."

The orchard gate creaked open and Jasmine turned to see her mom coming in.

"He's looking beautiful, Jasmine," she said.

"He is, isn't he?" said Jasmine, stroking him fondly.

"I'm afraid I've come with bad news," said Mom. "Mr. Hobson just called to say he's got a cold and he can't come today."

"No!" cried Jasmine. "He *has* to come."

Tom looked dismayed.

"I'm sorry," said Mom. "I know it's disappointing for you. He's upset not to be visiting, too, but he thinks it will be too much today, what with the nativity play this afternoon as well. I'll reschedule it for next Saturday. I'm sure he'll be better by then."

"He can't come next Saturday. He's going to stay at his daughter's for Christmas, remember?"

"Oh, yes, you're right. I'd forgotten. That's a shame."

"I promised they could see each other every week," said Jasmine, "and now it won't be until after Christmas."

"I'm really sorry, but there's nothing we can do about it. I'll make another arrangement for the earliest date I can."

Jasmine turned to Tom as her mother walked back to the house. "Poor Mr. Hobson. He'll be so sad."

Tom looked thoughtful. "I was reading about the Donkey Sanctuary in Devon. They take their donkeys to visit places like Holly Tree House. They say the donkeys and the older people really like it."

Jasmine stared at him. "Yes! Of course! We can take Mistletoe to Holly Tree House. If Mr. Hobson can't come here, we'll bring the donkey to him."

"Do you think they'd let us?"

"Well, you said the Donkey Sanctuary does."

"Yes, but I don't know if all assisted-living places let donkeys in."

Jasmine laid her face against the donkey's cheek. His coat was soft and warm.

"What if we didn't ask? What if we just took him? We can go this afternoon, after the nativity play."

Tom frowned. "But what if they won't let us in?"

"There'll be lots of people there. We should be able to sneak him in somehow. And if anyone from the home asks us what we're doing, we'll say he's part of the play."

"And if anyone from school asks us," said Tom, "we'll say it's been arranged as a surprise for the residents. And that's not a lie, because it has been arranged as a surprise. We don't need to say it was us who arranged it."

"Exactly," said Jasmine. "It's a foolproof plan."

11
The Donkey Costume

The two children and the donkey paused at the entrance to Holly Tree House. It was a big, grand house beside the town green, set back from the road behind wooden gates.

Tom let go of the lead rope and rubbed his gloved hands together. "It's freezing. I hope Mistletoe's not cold."

Jasmine put down the bucket she was carrying, pulled off a glove, and felt the donkey's back. "He feels warm. And his coat's so thick, I'm sure he's fine."

Tom looked at his watch. "We've got lots of time. They won't even have started the play yet. Let's have a look around and find the best way to take Mistletoe in."

They walked up the driveway to the front entrance. It had a wide porch with stone pillars. There was a keypad and a bell next to the door, which was firmly shut.

"They'll never let us in this way," said Tom. "Let's find another door. Walk on, Mistletoe."

"It's lucky you're not a noisy donkey," Jasmine said as they made their way along the front of the house. "We'd never be able to keep it a surprise if you started braying."

As they turned the corner, a woman in a uniform walked out of a side door, carrying a garbage bag. She closed the door behind her. Jasmine waited until she was out of sight and then tried the handle, hoping it wasn't one of those doors that locked automatically when you shut it.

The door opened. She grinned triumphantly

94

at Tom. She opened the door just wide enough to glimpse a long carpeted corridor with several doors opening off it. A buzz of excited children's voices came from one of the rooms. There was a burst of loud laughter. That was definitely Manu and Ben.

A door at the far end of the corridor opened and Ms. Denby, the teaching assistant, appeared. Behind her jostled a gaggle of girls in white dresses and tinsel halos.

"Now remember," said Ms. Denby, "we're going to walk quietly and calmly into the dining room, and we're all going to wait there until it's time to go into the residents' lounge to perform the play."

So we need to find out how to get into the residents' lounge, thought Jasmine. Mr. Hobson would be there to watch the play, and they could take Mistletoe to see him afterward.

Softly, she closed the door and told Tom what she had heard.

"Let's go around to the back," said Tom. "There might be a door into the lounge there. Walk on, Mistletoe."

Mistletoe was enjoying grazing on the lawn, but he obediently raised his head and plodded alongside them.

A paved terrace ran along the back of the house, with benches placed at intervals facing out across the lawn. Two sets of glass patio doors led onto the terrace.

"I'll take Mistletoe into those bushes while you look through the doors," said Tom, pointing to a clump of tall shrubs on the lawn. "See if one of those rooms is the lounge."

Jasmine walked over to the first set of glass doors. A climbing plant ran around the door frame. By positioning herself behind it, she could look in without being seen.

It was a large dining room, decorated for Christmas with paper chains looped from the ceiling and sprigs of holly tucked behind the pictures. The round tables were draped with pretty cloths and set for afternoon tea with plates and cups and saucers. Two old ladies sat at a table in the corner playing cards. Despite the cold outside, the little window above the patio doors was partly open.

Several people wearing uniforms appeared from a kitchen next to the dining room. They carried trays of party food, which they set on the tables. Jasmine's mouth watered at the sight of plates of sandwiches, bowls of chips, and three-tier

 97

cake stands heaped with scones spread with jam and cream, cupcakes, brownies, and all sorts of delicious-looking fancy cookies. A woman placed jugs of juice on each table while a man set out plastic cups.

Jasmine remembered Manu saying the younger students were going to have afternoon tea with the residents after the play. Lucky them.

The catering staff finished setting up the tea and left. The door from the corridor opened and Ms. Denby appeared with the angels. Their eyes lit up at the sight of the food. They pointed and grinned, and one of them started jumping up and down with excitement. Ms. Denby gave her a stern look.

"Matilda, that is not the sort of behavior we want, is it? We're going to walk through the room very carefully, and wait quietly by the door over there. Don't knock the tables, and don't touch *anything*."

Matilda stopped jumping and pursed her lips tightly together in an exaggerated display of obedience.

The angels filed through the room, looking longingly at the party food as they passed the tables. The shepherds and Wise Men followed them. One Wise Man snatched a chip when the teacher's back was turned. Ms. Denby started lining up the angels by a door on the other side of the room.

That door must lead to the lounge, thought Jasmine. *That's where we need to take Mistletoe.* Hopefully the other set of patio doors opened straight into the lounge. She wondered if they opened from the outside.

She was about to go investigate when there was a commotion in the crowd of shepherds. Something seemed to be jostling them from behind, making them screech and giggle, but the dining room was now so full of costumed children that Jasmine couldn't tell what was causing the disturbance.

Then she saw it, and her heart sank.

A small, misshapen pantomime donkey shoved its way through the shepherds and galloped clumsily around the room.

"Oh, no," whispered Jasmine.

"Manu! Ben! Stop!" shouted Mrs. Cowan, bursting through the doors behind them. But the donkey careened around the room, kicking up its heels. Ms. Denby blocked its path, but it veered to the side, knocking a table and toppling a jug. Pink juice poured onto the Angel Gabriel's white dress. She screamed and leaped backward, sending a chair crashing into the table. A cake stand toppled over, and scones and cookies skidded across the floor.

"Manu! Ben!" called Ms. Denby. "Stop that right now! Stand still!"

She tried to catch the donkey, but it wheeled around and galloped between the tables, sending chairs crashing to the floor. Its head now turned at an unnatural angle, and it no longer seemed to have any idea where it was going.

Mrs. Cowan, her mouth open in horror, wove her way between the tables toward the donkey. It turned and galloped off in the other direction. Mrs. Cowan followed it, shouting, "Stop! Manu! Ben! Stop!"

The donkey turned and crashed into the huddle of shepherds. Children dodged out of the way as it galumphed around the room, scattering sandwiches and sending jugs of juice pouring onto the floor.

Two of the catering staff appeared in the kitchen doorway. Their mouths opened in horror. Mrs. Cowan desperately battled through the sea of children to block the donkey's way. Just as it was about to crash into her, its back legs slipped in a puddle of juice. Its front legs skidded on a soggy sandwich and the donkey toppled sideways into a table. The cake stand clattered to the floor and the donkey collapsed in a tangle of hooves, landing facedown with its head in a heap of scones.

There was a terrible silence. The donkey struggled to its feet. Its face was covered in clotted cream. Chunks of squashed scone stuck to the cream like huge lumps. Its juice-soaked body and legs were dotted with soggy bits of broken cookies and squished chips.

The donkey slowly removed its head. And there, for the whole room to see, was the tousled hair and sweaty face of Jasmine's little brother.

12
Who's Going to Be the Donkey?

Jasmine couldn't bear to watch. She walked back to the bushes and told Tom what she'd seen.

"They're going to be in so much trouble," she said. "And those poor cooks. What a waste of a lovely tea."

"Do you think they'll cancel the play?" asked Tom.

Jasmine stared at him. It hadn't occurred to her that the play would be canceled.

"If they do," said Tom, "then we can just take

Mistletoe in to see the residents now, and I bet the head of the home will be really happy we brought him."

"I'll go and see what's happening," said Jasmine.

She took up her position beside the doors again. All the children except Manu and Ben had been herded to the end of the room nearest the lounge. One of the catering staff carried the donkey costume into the kitchen. Manu and Ben stood on their own in the middle of the room, looking very subdued. The two card-playing ladies in the corner had their heads turned, apparently talking to somebody behind them. Jasmine craned her neck to see.

Harrison was crouched behind the table with his hands over his ears. The old ladies were clearly trying to comfort him, but Harrison was shaking his head from side to side and shrinking farther into the corner. Ms. Denby, who normally helped him, was sponging juice off the Angel Gabriel on the other side of the room.

Poor Harrison, thought Jasmine. *He must have hated all that chaos.*

Ms. Denby finished with the Angel Gabriel and straightened up. She turned and spotted Harrison behind the table. With a look of concern, she hurried over to a chair by the wall, fished Harrison's headphones out of a bag, and took them to him. Harrison put them on, but he shook his head and stayed crouched in the corner when Ms. Denby held out her hand to encourage him to stand up.

Suddenly, Jasmine had an idea. It might not work, but it was worth a try. She pushed down the door handle and slipped inside the room.

The teachers had their backs to Jasmine, but one of the shepherds recognized her and waved. Jasmine put her finger to her lips and crept in an exaggerated tiptoe toward Harrison. The children took the hint and said nothing. Some of them even put their fingers to their lips, too.

Manu was pleading with Mrs. Cowan. He sounded close to tears.

"Please," he begged. "We'll be so good, I promise. We'll do everything you tell us, won't we, Ben? *Please*, Mrs. Cowan. We'll do anything."

"Absolutely not," said Mrs. Cowan. "I just can't trust you. You were given very clear instructions and you did exactly what you were told not to do."

Jasmine squeezed behind the corner table and crouched beside Harrison. His eyes were screwed shut and he was rocking backward and forward.

"Harrison," she whispered. "It's me, Jasmine."

He kept rocking.

"Harrison," whispered Jasmine. "Mistletoe is here."

His rocking slowed a little.

"Mistletoe is right outside," said Jasmine. "Do you want to come and see him?"

He hovered his hands slightly away from his ears and opened his eyes.

"Mistletoe," he murmured.

"Come and see him. Come and see Mistletoe."

"Mistletoe," said Harrison. He lowered his hands.

"He's in the garden, just outside that door."

She held out her hand. Without looking at her, he took it and got to his feet. The old ladies smiled at her as she led him toward the patio doors.

Mrs. Cowan was giving instructions to Manu and Ben.

"You will sit on the floor at the front and watch the play. I'll be keeping an eye on you the entire time, so do not move a muscle."

"But who's going to be the donkey?" asked Ben.

"Nobody is going to be the donkey."

"But what about when everyone sings 'Little Donkey,'" said Manu. "It won't make sense if there isn't a donkey."

As Jasmine glimpsed her brother's crestfallen face, she felt a pang of sympathy. Poor Manu. He had been so looking forward to playing the donkey. She and Harrison slipped outside and Jasmine closed the door behind them, shuddering as the freezing air hit her. Harrison smiled in delight as he saw the donkey grazing on the lawn.

"Mistletoe," he said. The donkey raised his head and swiveled his ears toward him. Harrison put his arms around Mistletoe's neck and leaned his head against the donkey's mane.

"What's happening in there?" Tom asked Jasmine.

"Manu and Ben aren't allowed to be the donkey anymore."

"So who is?"

"No one. They're not having a donkey."

"That's a shame. It won't be as good without a donkey."

Harrison raised his head and looked at Jasmine. "Mistletoe," he said.

"Yes," said Jasmine absently.

"Mistletoe," repeated Harrison, and the urgency of his tone made Jasmine take notice.

"Oh!" she breathed. "Mistletoe. Of course!"

Tom stared at her, and then at Harrison.

"Do you mean Mistletoe should be the donkey in the play?"

Harrison nodded.

Jasmine and Tom looked at each other, and their faces broke into smiles.

"That's a great idea," said Tom. "Of course it should be Mistletoe. Imagine how pleased Mr. Hobson will be to see him in the play!"

"But how are we going to do it?" asked Jasmine. "The play's about to start."

"Harrison will need to lead him," said Tom. "Will you do that, Harrison?"

Harrison nodded.

"Right," said Jasmine. "Let's make a plan."

13
The Nativity Play

From the lounge drifted the sound of "O Come All Ye Faithful," played softly on a piano. Jasmine looked through the glass doors. Dozens of children were crowded at this end of the room, all facing the stage at the front. The boy and girl playing Mary and Joseph stood at the back of the crowd, just on the other side of the door from Jasmine.

She noticed with gratitude that there was a window open in this room, too, so she would be able to hear what was happening.

Over the heads of the costumed children, Jasmine saw the residents of Holly Tree House waiting for the play to begin. They sat in armchairs and wheelchairs, with a central aisle between the chairs for the performers to walk down. The front of the room had been left clear as a stage. A dark-blue backdrop, painted with a scene of Bethlehem by night under a starry sky, hung on the wall behind the stage.

Mr. Hobson was sitting on his own at the side of the room. He looked tired from his move and his cold. It was sad to see him here instead of out in his field with Mistletoe. There he had been busy running a farm. Jasmine hoped Holly Tree House had fun activities.

Jasmine walked back to the others.

"It looks like they're about to start. Let's wait on the terrace until it's time for Mary and Joseph to come on. Then we'll open the doors and Harrison and Mistletoe can walk down the aisle with them."

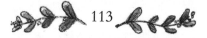

"Shouldn't we warn Mary and Joseph?" said Tom. "They might get a bit of a shock if a donkey suddenly appears beside them with no warning."

"Good point," said Jasmine. "I'll creep in and tell them."

The angels were processing up the aisle, singing "O Little Town of Bethlehem," accompanied by the piano. Jasmine inched open the door. The children at the back turned as the cold air hit them. One of the Wise Men gave a little scream, which luckily was drowned out by the piano and the appreciative murmurs of the audience as the angels approached the stage.

Mrs. Cowan stood at the side of the stage, smiling encouragingly at the angels. Ms. Denby was at the back of the room, facing away from Jasmine, lining up the shepherds.

Jasmine beckoned to Mary and Joseph. They looked bemused, but they knew she was Manu's big sister and they followed her without questioning.

Outside, Jasmine shut the door behind them and pointed across the lawn, where Harrison was leading Mistletoe toward the terrace.

The children gasped. "A donkey!" said Joseph.

"He's so cute!" said Mary.

"He's going to be in the play with you," said Jasmine. "He's called Mistletoe and he's my donkey. Harrison's going to lead him up the aisle, and you can walk with him, exactly like you were

 115

going to walk with the pretend donkey. Is that OK?"

Mary and Joseph beamed.

"Can I pet him?" asked Mary.

"Sure," said Jasmine. "Harrison will show you where he likes being petted."

"What if he poops?" asked Joseph.

"He probably won't, but we've got a bucket just in case. Actually, can you carry it? Stand it under his back end when he gets onstage. If he moves, move the bucket, too."

"Oh!" gasped Tom. "It's snowing!"

Jasmine looked up. Fat white snowflakes drifted like magic from the winter sky.

"Yay!" she exclaimed. "Snow!"

Mary and Joseph laughed and clapped in delight. "Snow!"

"Look, Mistletoe, snow!" said Harrison, throwing back his head and opening his mouth to catch the falling flakes, laughing as they melted on his tongue.

They led Mistletoe onto the terrace, Mary and Joseph running with their hands held out wide to catch snowflakes.

As they reached the doors, the angels finished singing. Four children who Jasmine guessed were narrators walked up the aisle. They wore Christmas sweaters instead of costumes, and each clutched a clipboard with a script attached to it.

The first narrator, a very confident-looking boy in a snowman sweater, yelled, "WELCOME TO OUR NATIVITY PLAY!"

The audience jumped as though they had been given electric shocks. A few people started laughing.

Jasmine turned to check on Harrison. He stood beside Mistletoe, murmuring the donkey's name over and over again. And while Mistletoe's left ear was swiveling around, listening to the noises from inside, his right ear was fixed on Harrison.

The second narrator said, "The Angel Gabriel was sent from God to a city called Nazareth, to a young woman named Mary, who was engaged to a man called Joseph."

 118

The Angel Gabriel stepped forward and said, "Do not be afraid, Mary. God is with you. You will have a baby and you will call him Jesus, and he will be the Son of God."

One of the angels was picking her nose and inspecting the results with intense interest. One had sat down with her legs crossed and appeared to be taking a nap. Another was looking around the audience anxiously. Suddenly her face broke into a beaming smile and she ran off down the aisle calling, "Nana! Nana!"

Mrs. Cowan whispered to the third narrator, who lifted his clipboard and held it directly in front of his face. In one breathless outpouring, he gabbled, "In those days, Caesar Augustus ordered that everyone must go to be registered in their own town. So Mary and Joseph went to Bethlehem."

The piano started to play "Little Donkey." Mary and Joseph looked at Jasmine expectantly.

Until this moment, Jasmine had been so caught

119

up in the excitement of their plan that she hadn't considered the possible consequences. Now her stomach twisted into knots.

Feeling queasy, she opened the double doors wide.

"Ready, Harrison?" she whispered.

"Walk on," said Harrison.

He began to lead Mistletoe up the aisle beside Mary and Joseph. Mistletoe kept his right ear trained on Harrison, and Jasmine could tell that Harrison was murmuring the donkey's name. Mrs. Cowan stared, openmouthed and speechless. Jasmine and Tom hastily ducked behind the Wise Men.

A wave of gasps and murmurs rose around the room as the little procession made its way up the aisle.

"Ahh!"

"Oh, look!"

"A real donkey!"

"Isn't he beautiful?"

"Look at that, George, a real donkey."

"What a sweet little creature."

"Look at his dear little face."

Jasmine couldn't resist standing up to look at Mr. Hobson. He was gazing at Mistletoe as though he was in a trance.

Most of the angels had stopped singing "Little Donkey" and were staring openmouthed at Mistletoe as he walked calmly up the aisle, one ear swiveling and the other trained on Harrison. Jasmine noticed Manu and Ben grinning in delight at Harrison and Mistletoe.

They reached the stage and turned to face the audience. The music stopped and there was an expectant hush. Then, just as the fourth narrator opened his mouth to speak, a voice came from the side of the room.

"Mistletoe," said Mr. Hobson hoarsely. "It's my Mistletoe."

The donkey's ears swiveled toward him. Mr. Hobson tried to heave himself out of his wheelchair, but he seemed too tired and sank down again.

"Mistletoe," he said croakily.

Mistletoe lifted his head and brayed. Then he trotted off the stage and over to Mr. Hobson,

with Harrison beside him. He laid his head in the
old man's lap. Mr. Hobson's face lit up in a huge
smile. He rested his head against the donkey's and
scratched his ears.

"Mistletoe," he murmured. "My Mistletoe."

14

The Best Christmas Surprise

Jasmine beckoned to Tom to follow her, and they crawled on their hands and knees around the back of the audience until they were just behind Mr. Hobson. He hadn't seen them yet, and they kept quiet. Jasmine didn't want to cause any more commotion. Harrison held Mistletoe's lead rope loosely, while Mistletoe rested his head in Mr. Hobson's lap and Mr. Hobson scratched him behind the ears.

At the end of the play, as the final verse of

"Away in a Manger" finished, applause broke out around the room. Everyone was smiling.

A woman who had been sitting at the front stood up and walked to the stage.

"Good afternoon, everyone. For those of you who don't know me, my name's Katy Bright, and I'm the manager of Holly Tree House. On behalf of all of us here, I want to say a huge thank you to all of you, children and teachers, for coming here and performing your play for us. We're so grateful to you for giving us this lovely Christmas treat. And we certainly didn't expect to have a real donkey in our midst. Thank you so much, Mrs. Cowan, for organizing that fantastic surprise."

She smiled at Mrs. Cowan, who looked rather flustered.

"Now, even though we had a little mishap before the show, our wonderful kitchen staff have performed a Christmas miracle and there's a beautiful tea ready in the dining room. Children, if you could just stay in here for a tiny bit longer while we get all the residents seated next door, then I'll ask you to come and join us."

Mrs. Cowan sat the children in rows on the stage while the staff helped the residents into the dining room. When a man came over to Mr. Hobson, though, he shook his head.

"I'll stay here," he said. "With my donkey, and my helper here." He smiled at Harrison.

"You must be Harrison," he said when the caregiver left. "Is that right?"

Harrison nodded.

"Jasmine told me how good you are with Mistletoe. You handled him beautifully there. With all those people around, he might have panicked, but you kept him completely calm. He really trusts you."

Harrison leaned his head against the donkey's flank.

"How did you get him here?" asked Mr. Hobson. "Did you bring him yourself?"

Harrison shook his head and pointed at Jasmine.

 126

Jasmine jumped to her feet and stood in front of Mr. Hobson. "We brought him," she said. "Me and Tom."

Tom stood up, grinning.

"We were sad that you couldn't come see Mistletoe today," said Jasmine, "so we thought we'd bring him here, as a surprise for you after the play. And then Manu and Ben went wild in the donkey costume so they weren't allowed to be in the play, and Harrison had the idea of Mistletoe being in it instead."

Mr. Hobson beamed at them all. "You're a wonderful bunch of children," he said. "I couldn't believe my eyes when I saw Mistletoe walk up that aisle. I honestly thought I was seeing things for a moment. It's the best Christmas surprise I've ever had."

Jasmine fetched Mr. Hobson a plate of food, but he didn't have a chance to eat anything because a steady stream of people kept coming up to pet Mistletoe and ask him about the donkey. After half an hour, he could barely speak, and a concerned-looking caregiver asked him if he wanted to go rest in his room.

"No, no," he croaked. "I've been doing nothing but resting all week. I'm having a wonderful time."

And despite his cold and his hoarse voice, he

looked years younger than he had before the play. His face was animated and he was clearly loving the attention. The two ladies who had been playing cards in the dining room made their way over. One had a little bag filled with carrot and apple pieces dangling from her walker.

"Lovely Maeve in the kitchen gave us these for your little donkey," said the taller of the ladies. "We thought he might be hungry."

"Is he your donkey, Ted?" asked her friend. "How come you've got a donkey?"

Mr. Hobson told them he was a farmer, and they started asking all sorts of questions about his farm and his animals while Mistletoe munched contentedly on his snacks.

"Uh-oh," said Tom, nudging Jasmine. "Now we're in for it."

Mrs. Cowan had caught Jasmine's eye a while ago, but she had been fully occupied with supervising her class. Jasmine had hoped she and Tom would be able to slip away before the teacher

129

managed to give them her attention. Now, though, Mrs. Cowan and the manager of Holly Tree House were heading purposefully toward them.

"Hello, Jasmine," said Mrs. Cowan. Her face gave nothing away. "Hello, Tom. Mrs. Bright would like a word with you."

Oh, no. This was worse than she'd thought. She could cope with being scolded by Mrs. Cowan, but to be scolded by a stranger was a much more horrible prospect.

Much to her surprise, though, Mrs. Bright smiled at them.

"Is this your donkey, Jasmine?" she asked.

"Yes," said Jasmine, feeling a bit queasy. "But he used to be Mr. Hobson's. Well, he still is, really. He belongs to both of us. And Mr. Hobson was supposed to be coming to visit him this morning, but then he couldn't. So we brought Mistletoe here. We'd heard about donkeys visiting retirement places, so we thought we'd do it, too. We

 130

didn't really have time to let you know before we came."

"That's exactly what I wanted to talk to you about," said Mrs. Bright. "I've read about donkeys visiting homes as well, and I thought it was a lovely idea, but I didn't know of anywhere local with donkeys. But here you are, and everyone is loving Mistletoe's visit. He seems to have the ideal temperament for it."

"Oh, yes," said Jasmine. "He loves company and he's really gentle."

"We wondered if you'd like to bring him to visit on a regular basis," said Mrs. Bright. "You'd need an adult to come with you, but perhaps one of your parents wouldn't mind?"

Jasmine could hardly believe what she was hearing.

"That would be great," she said. "My parents are going to bring Mr. Hobson to the farm anyway, so I'm sure sometimes we could bring Mistletoe here instead."

She stepped over to the donkey and scratched him behind the ears. "Would you like that, Mistletoe?" she asked.

Mistletoe dipped his head down and raised it again. Tom laughed.

"He's nodding!" he said. "Mistletoe agrees."

When Jasmine heard familiar voices in the dining room, she grabbed Tom's arm and dragged him behind the Bethlehem backdrop.

"Hey, what are you doing?" he said.

"My parents! They've come to pick up Manu. I forgot."

"You should have dragged Mistletoe behind the curtain, not me. I think he might give us away."

"Right, let's grab him and go. Hopefully they won't even come into—oh, no, too late."

Jasmine's parents walked into the lounge. They stopped in their tracks, looking utterly confused, as they saw Mistletoe standing with Mr. Hobson and Mrs. Bright.

"It's not like we've actually done anything wrong," said Tom. "We only brought Mistletoe to visit his friend."

Jasmine strained to hear what the adults were saying, but there was too much noise in the room. Then Mr. Hobson spotted her and Tom peeping out from behind the backdrop. He laughed and beckoned them over.

They gave each other a nervous glance and emerged from their hiding place. As they crossed the room, they were nearly knocked down by Manu, bounding toward his parents. His face was all smiles.

"Mrs. Cowan says me and Ben can still be the

134

donkey when we do the play for the town! So you and Ella will get to see us."

"Ah, yes," said Dad. "Mrs. Cowan had a word with us about that. It seems it was lucky there was an alternative donkey on hand today."

Jasmine squirmed as her parents turned their eyes on her.

"These three have done so well with Mistletoe," said Mr. Hobson, indicating Jasmine, Tom, and Harrison. "They've given him a whole new lease on life."

"You must be very proud of your daughter," said Mrs. Bright. "She has such initiative."

Mom raised her eyebrows. "Well, that's one word for it."

Mr. Hobson chuckled. "I bet you never get bored with Jasmine and Manu around. You're very lucky to have them."

Mom smiled at Dad. "I suppose we are. All things considered, I suppose we are."

"And they're lucky to have you," said Mr. Hobson.

"Mostly, though," said Jasmine, "we're lucky to have Mistletoe."

Mr. Hobson smiled. "I can't disagree with that," he said, scratching Mistletoe's withers. "We're all lucky to have Mistletoe."

Turn the page for
a quiz and a sneak peek of
the next book in the
JASMINE GREEN RESCUES series!

🐴 Quiz: All About Donkeys! 🐴

Try taking this quiz to see how much
you've learned about donkeys from reading
A Donkey Called Mistletoe.

1. What might you say to a donkey if you want it to start moving forward?

a. Move on

b. Come on

c. Walk on

d. Go on

2. Why do donkeys need a shelter in their field?

a. Because they get cold in the winter

b. Because their fur isn't waterproof

c. Because they're scared of the dark

d. Because they get sunstroke in the heat

3. Where on a donkey are its withers?

a. At the top of the shoulders

b. At the ankles

c. At the knees

d. Just above the tail

4. **Which of these behaviors shows that a donkey is relaxed?**

   a. Swishing its tail
   b. Stamping its foot
   c. Flattening its ears back
   d. Pointing its ears forward

5. **What is the name of the stiff brush used for getting dried mud and dirt out of a donkey's coat?**

   a. A handy brush
   b. A sandy brush
   c. A dandy brush
   d. A candy brush

6. **What might you say to a donkey if you want it to stop moving?**

   a. Stop
   b. Stay
   c. Freeze
   d. Halt

Jasmine Green
Rescues
A Foal
Called Storm

1
Where Have You Come From?

"That was a massive storm last night," said Jasmine to her sheepdog as she clambered over a fallen tree branch. "Did the thunder scare you, Sky?"

Sky leaped over the branch and ran along the riverbank, wagging his fluffy tail. If he had been frightened by the thunder, he showed no sign of it this morning.

It was the last Tuesday of May, and the school year had just finished. Jasmine had gotten up early, as usual, and had fed her other animals before walking Sky. She needed to be organized today because she had two rabbits coming to stay for the rest of the week.

Jasmine sometimes looked after other people's pets when they went on vacation. The money she made helped to pay for her animals' food. It was also good experience because she was planning to have an animal rescue center and boarding facility when she grew up.

They were almost back at the farmhouse when Jasmine heard a strange sound. Frowning in confusion, she stopped and listened.

The farm was full of noises: birds singing in the hedgerows, sheep baaing in the meadows, roosters crowing in the yard.

But this was different. It was a high-pitched whinny. None of the animals on Oak Tree Farm sounded like that.

Jasmine walked past the farmhouse toward the field called the Sixteen Acres, where the sound seemed to have come from. There were no animals there at the moment.

And then she stopped and stared in amazement.

Standing beside the hedge was a beautiful chestnut foal. It had a white blaze on its face and white socks on its hind legs. As Jasmine stared in amazement, it lifted its head and gave another high-pitched whinny.

What was a foal doing there?

Jasmine's heart raced as the possibilities ran through her head. Her mom was a vet. Maybe she had brought the foal to the farm to recover after an illness or an operation. She had never done that before, but it was possible.

But if she had, then why hadn't she mentioned it? Suddenly a truly thrilling thought struck Jasmine.

What if the foal was a present? Had Mom and Dad actually bought her a foal of her own?

Her excitement drained away as she considered this in more detail. She already had two cats, a pig, a duck, a sheepdog, a ram, a deer, and a donkey. Apart from her cats, Toffee and Marmite, Jasmine had rescued all these animals. And she had always had to fight her parents in order to keep them. Every time, they reminded her how many animals she already had, how much they cost to feed, how much space they needed, and how much time it took to look after them.

But Jasmine was an optimist. Although it was unlikely, it wasn't impossible. She clipped on Sky's leash and slowly approached the field.

The field gate was wide open, and suddenly Jasmine understood how ridiculous her hopes were. Even if her parents *had* bought her the foal, they certainly wouldn't have left it alone in a field with the gate open.

So whose was it, and where had it come from?

As she drew closer, she saw that something was very wrong.

The foal was soaking wet. It must have been out in that terrible storm that had blown through. The foal was shivering all over, which could have been from the cold, but looked more like fear.

Its nostrils flared and quivered, and the whites of its eyes were showing. Its tail was clamped down against its body. Its ears swiveled rapidly, flicking back and forth, as though it was about to flee at any moment.

Jasmine stopped several yards away and spoke in a soft murmur, trying to soothe the little creature.

"What's wrong, little foal? Are you lost? Where's your mom?"

The foal was beautiful, with big dark eyes, a short mane and tail, and long legs. As Jasmine softly approached, it backed away, terrified. She noticed it was limping.

"Oh! You're hurt!"

There was a nasty cut on the foal's hind leg. The gaping wound looked recent, and there was a lot of dried blood around it.

"You poor thing. What happened to you?"

The wound looked deep enough to need stitches. That was a job for Mom, but she was out on an emergency call.

Jasmine thought quickly. An animal as nervous as this might bolt if anything startled it. She needed to keep the foal safe, but it was far too jumpy to let her approach it. She would just have to shut it in the field.

"I'm going to close this," she said as she walked slowly and quietly to the gate. "Don't worry, you're safe now. I'll look after you."

Jasmine had never cared for a foal before, but she had dealt with other frightened animals. She stood by the gate, speaking gently, trying to reassure the trembling creature.

"You're a boy, aren't you? I wonder what your name is. Do you even have a name? Are you an orphan? Are you hungry?"

If only Mom were here. But even if she were, she wouldn't be able to treat the foal's wound when he was this nervous. He would bolt if anyone went near him and probably give himself another injury.

Suddenly Jasmine knew what she needed to do.

"I'll fetch some rails and build you a pen. That's what Mom does if she treats an animal in the field. And I'll phone Tom to come and help. He'll be so excited to meet you."

She took Sky back to the house and phoned Tom. He was Jasmine's best friend, and they had rescued many animals together. He lived very close to Oak Tree Farm, so he and Jasmine could walk to each other's houses.

"That's amazing," he said. "I'll come over right away."

Jasmine fetched metal rails from the lambing barn and carried them to the field one by one. As she approached the gate, the foal backed away, trembling. His ears were pinned back. Jasmine knew from experience with her donkey, Mistletoe, that this was another sign of anxiety.

When she opened the gate, the foal cocked his hind hoof, preparing to kick.

"Thanks for the warning," she said. "I'll stay far away from your back legs." As she carried the last rail in, Tom walked into the field.

"He's so beautiful!" he said. "I can't believe he just turned up here."

"I know. But he's so scared, poor baby. Look how he's shivering."

"Do you think he ran away? How did he get that horrible cut?"

"I don't know, but something bad must have happened to him. He's way too young to be away from his mom."

"Have you phoned the police?"

Jasmine didn't want to admit she hadn't thought of this. "Mom will phone them when she gets home," she said.

"Maybe he was abandoned," said Tom. "Or stolen."

"He can't have been stolen. If he was, the thieves would have him, wouldn't they? They wouldn't have left him here."

"Unless he escaped," said Tom.

While they constructed the pen, they talked

softly to the foal, hoping to get him to relax and start to trust them.

"His coat's a lovely color," said Tom. "I like his white socks, too."

"And those cute little white markings on his forelegs, just above his hooves," said Jasmine.

By the time they'd finished, the foal had stopped trembling, but his mouth was tight and pinched and his body was still rigid with stress.

"How are we going to get him into the pen?" Tom asked.

"I'm not sure. When Mom treats foals, she always gets their mother to lead them in. They follow their moms anywhere."

"What about putting some food in there?"

"I don't know what to give him," said Jasmine. "He looks too young for solid food and I don't know if it's safe to give him cow's milk."

"Can you phone your mom?"

"Not really. She's probably delivering a calf right now."

From the orchard came a loud braying sound. The little foal pricked up his ears.

Tom's eyes widened. "What about Mistletoe?"

"To lead him into the pen?"

"Yes. Maybe the foal would follow him."

Jasmine looked doubtful. "He's not going to think Mistletoe's his mom."

"No, but horses and donkeys usually get along, don't they? Mr. Hobson said people have donkeys as companions for their horses, and some people use them as babysitters for foals."

Mr. Hobson was Mistletoe's previous owner, and he knew everything about donkeys.

"Well, if anyone can calm him down, it will be Mistletoe," said Jasmine. "He's the kindest donkey in the whole world."

Which animals have you helped Jasmine rescue?

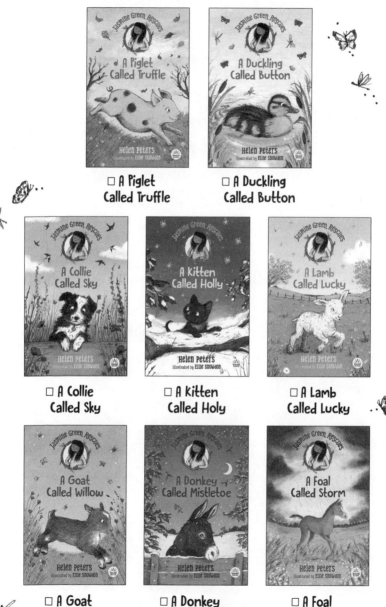

☐ A Piglet
Called Truffle

☐ A Duckling
Called Button

☐ A Collie
Called Sky

☐ A Kitten
Called Holy

☐ A Lamb
Called Lucky

☐ A Goat
Called Willow

☐ A Donkey
Called Mistletoe

☐ A Foal
Called Storm

About the Creators

Helen Peters is the author of numerous books for young readers that feature heroic girls saving the day on farms. She grew up on an old-fashioned farm in England, surrounded by family, animals, and mud. Helen Peters lives in London.

Ellie Snowdon is a children's author–illustrator from a tiny village in South Wales. She received her MA in children's book illustration at Cambridge School of Art. Ellie Snowdon lives in Cambridge, England.